# Look and Learn

## A First Book about

# Patterns

The original publishers would like to thank the following children
for modeling for this book: Daisy Bartlett, Chilli Bernstein,
April Cain, Milo Clare, Safari George, Jack Matthews,
Rebekah Murrell, Giovanni Sipiano.

**For a free color catalog describing Gareth Stevens
Publishing's list of high-quality books and multimedia
programs, call 1-800-542-2595 (USA) or 1-800-461-9120
(Canada). Gareth Stevens Publishing's Fax: (414) 225-0377.**

**Library of Congress Cataloging-in-Publication Data**

Tuxworth, Nicola.
    A first book about patterns / by Nicola Tuxworth.
       p. cm. — (Look and learn)
    Includes bibliographical references and index.
    Summary: Points out stripes, dots, wiggles, spirals,
and other patterns found in nature, clothes, food, and
objects around us.
    ISBN 0-8368-2288-9 (lib. bdg.)
    1. Pattern perception—Juvenile literature. [1. Pattern
perception.] I. Title. II. Series: Tuxworth, Nicola.
Look and learn.
BF311.T84   1999
152.14'23—dc21              98-31774

This North American edition first published in 1999 by
**Gareth Stevens Publishing**
1555 North RiverCenter Drive, Suite 201
Milwaukee, WI 53212 USA

Original edition © 1997 by Anness Publishing Limited.
First published in 1997 by Lorenz Books, an imprint
of Anness Publishing Inc., New York, New York.
This U.S. edition © 1999 by Gareth Stevens, Inc.
Additional end matter © 1999 by Gareth Stevens, Inc.

Editor: Sophie Warne
Special Photography: John Freeman
Stylist: Neil Hadfield
Design and typesetting: Liz Black

Picture credits: Holt Studios International: 17tl and b;
Papilio Photographic: 16b; Planet Earth Pictures: 17 tr;
Trip: 14br; Warren Photographic: 16t; Zefa: 15tl.

Printed in Mexico

1 2 3 4 5 6 7 8 9 03 02 01 00 99

# Look and Learn

## A First Book about

# Patterns

Nicola Tuxworth

Gareth Stevens Publishing
**MILWAUKEE**

# Stripes

Striped patterns are made from lines of different colors.

striped ball

striped candy canes

striped shorts

Look at all my different stripes!

**striped birthday present**

**striped pencil**

Who's behind the striped curtain?

**striped mugs**

5

# Spots

Spotted patterns are made from round dots.

**spotted handkerchief**

I'm spotted all over!

**pair of spotted dice**

**spotted purse**

spotted
bow tie

spotted
bugs

spotted party
balloons

spotted
cushion

7

# Checks

Checked patterns are made from squares.

**checked cushion**

Check out my outfit!

**checked wall tile**

**checked dinner plate**

# Plaid

Plaid patterns are made from crisscrossing stripes.

plaid kilt

plaid bag

plaid ribbon

plaid suspenders

My plaid pajamas are warm and cozy!

# Zigzags

Zigzag patterns are made from straight lines with sharp turns in them.

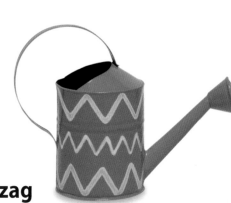

**zigzag watering can**

Do you like my amazing zigzag hat?

**zigzag picture frame**

**zigzag cookie**

# Wiggles

Wiggly patterns are made from wavy lines.

wiggly braid

wiggly toothpaste

wiggly box

I've got wiggles under my chin.

wiggly plate

# Swirls

Swirled patterns are made from twisting, curling lines.

**swirled china mug**

**swirled cream**

**swirled folder**

**swirled coffeepot**

# Spirals

Spiral patterns are made from lines that coil around and around.

**spiral china cat**

My spiral skirt is called a sarong.

**spiral spinning top**

**spiral cake**

# Natural patterns

There are many different patterns in nature.

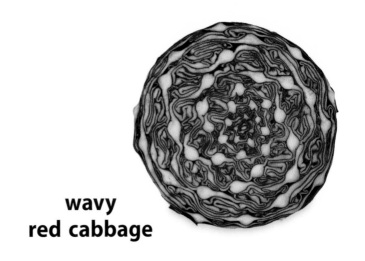

**wavy red cabbage**

**speckled eggs**

**speckled leaves**

**ripples of sand**

**spiral seashells**

**crisscrossing spiderweb**

**spotted pink lily**

Count the rings to find out the age of this tree.

15

# Animal patterns

Lots of animals have patterns on their bodies.

**scaly patterns on a fish**

**black-and-white stripes on zebras**

**zigzag patterns
on a snake**

**patchy patterns
on a giraffe**

Which patterns
can you see here?

# More patterns

Have you ever
seen any
patterns
like these?

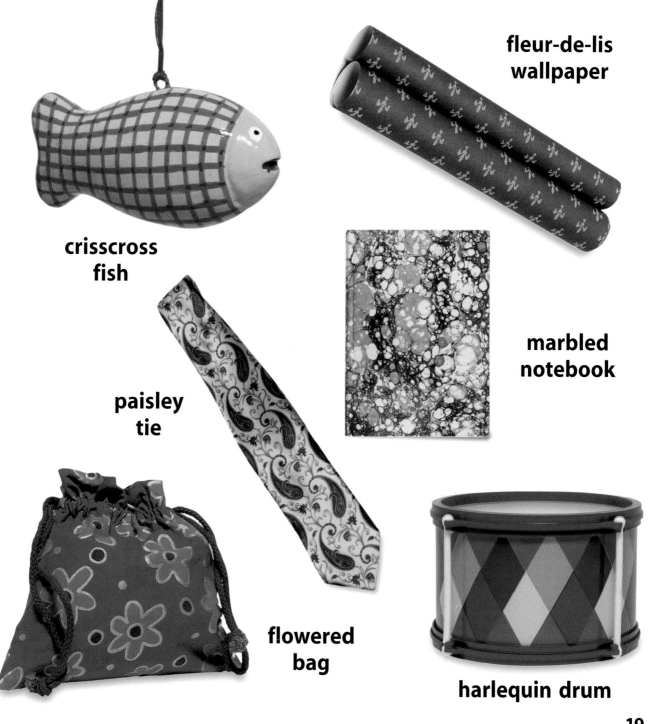

**fleur-de-lis wallpaper**

**crisscross fish**

**marbled notebook**

**paisley tie**

**flowered bag**

**harlequin drum**

# Making patterns

Try making some of these patterns.

drizzled icing

splotches of messy paint

zigzags in wet sand

I like making patterns with my feet!

**ripples in water**

Which patterns can you make?

21

# Name that pattern!

## Which patterns do you see?

# Glossary/Index

**fleur-de-lis:** an artistic design in the shape of an iris. (p. 19)

**harlequin:** a pattern with different-colored, diamond patches. (p. 19)

**kilt:** a traditional skirt sometimes worn by men in Scotland. (p. 9)

**plaid:** a pattern that is made up of stripes of different colors and widths that cross each other. (p. 9)

**ripples:** waves that are formed on the surface of water, for example, when an object falls into the water. (pp. 14, 21)

**sarong:** a kind of loose skirt that is made by wrapping cloth around the lower part of the body. (p. 13)

**scaly:** covered with thin plates, like the skin of a snake. (p. 16)

**speckled:** covered with spots. (p. 14)

# More Books to Read

*Dots, Spots, Speckles, and Stripes.* Tana Hoban (Greenwillow Books)

*Is It Shiny? Science Buzzwords (series).* Karen Bryant-Mole (Gareth Stevens)

*Spotty Animals.* Angela Wilkes (Dorling Kindersley)

*Zink the Zebra.* Kelly Weil (Gareth Stevens)

# Videos

*Bill Cosby's Picture Pages Shapes & Colors.* (Front Row Video)

*Colors & Shapes.* (Good Time Home Video)

# Web Sites

www.sesamestreet.org/

www.funschool.com/

Some web sites stay current longer than others. For further web sites, use your search engines to locate the following topics: *animal camouflage* and *patterns*.